# THE TWELVE DANCING PRINCESSES

*(A Folk Tale from the Brothers Grimm)*

Retold by Freya Littledale
Pictures by Isadore Seltzer

### SCHOLASTIC INC.
NEW YORK  TORONTO  LONDON  AUCKLAND  SYDNEY

Once upon a time there was a king
who had twelve beautiful daughters.
They slept in twelve beds
side by side in one room.
Every night the king took care
to lock the door.
Yet every morning he found
his daughters' dancing shoes
worn to pieces.

"How can this be?" cried the king.

But his daughters would tell him nothing.
And no one could discover their secret.

So the king sent this message
far and wide:

> He who finds out
> where my twelve daughters go
> will be the next king of the land.
> And he may choose a princess to wed.
> But if three nights pass
> and he does not know,
> then I will give one command—
> and that man shall lose his head.

Soon a prince came to the palace.
"I will find out your daughters' secret,"
he told the king.

So that night there was a wonderful feast,
and the prince was the guest of honor.
Then he was led to a room
next to the twelve princesses.

"I will leave their door open,"
said the king.
"You will hear what they say
and see where they go."

"Indeed I will," said the prince.
But his eyes began to close
and he fell into a deep sleep.
When he awoke in the morning
he found twenty-four dancing shoes
worn through and through.

"I will learn the secret yet,"
thought the prince.

But the same thing happened
the second night and the third.
Then the prince was brought before the king.
"Do you know where my daughters go
every night?" asked the king.

"No I don't," said the prince.
So the king gave his command.
And the prince was put to death.
Many others tried to learn
the secret of the dancing shoes.
But all of them failed.
And all of them lost their heads.

Now it happened that a poor soldier,
who had been wounded
and could no longer fight,
was walking through the forest
near the king's palace.

Along the way he met an old woman.
"Where are you going?" she asked him.

"I'm not sure," said the soldier.
"But wouldn't it be a lucky thing
  if I learned the secret of the dancing shoes?
  Then I would have a wife,
  and one day I would be king."

"It's really very easy," said the old woman.
"If a princess brings you wine before you go to bed,
  just pretend to drink it.
  Then pretend to sleep."

"Is that all?" asked the soldier.

"Not quite," said the old woman.
  And she gave him an old black cloak.
"The moment you put this on,
  you will become invisible.
  Then you can follow the princesses
  wherever they go.
  You will see them,
  but they won't see you."

"Thank you," said the soldier.
"Now I really will speak to the king."

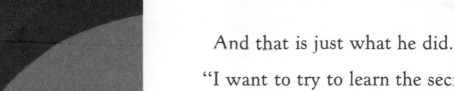

And that is just what he did.

"I want to try to learn the secret
of the dancing shoes," said he.

"Very well," said the king.
And he ordered some royal clothes for the soldier,
who looked just as grand as any prince
once he put them on.

That night, after a fine feast,
the soldier was led to the room
next to the twelve princesses.

Soon the eldest princess came
with a cup of wine.
"Drink this," said she,
"and you shall have sweet dreams."

But the soldier had tied a sponge
under his chin.
And down went the wine
straight into the sponge.
He did not drink a single drop.
Then he pretended to snore
his loudest snore.
"ZZZZZZZZZZZZZZZZZZZZZZZZ!"

The princesses laughed and rose from their beds.
"He will lose his head
just like the others," said the eldest.

At once they dressed in gowns of satin and lace
with dancing shoes to match.
They stood before the mirror,
brushed their beautiful hair,
and put on necklaces and rings.
All of them were happy
except the youngest princess.
"I don't know why,
but I'm frightened tonight," she said.

"Little goose!" said the eldest.
"You're always frightened.
None of the princes learned our secret.
What makes you think the soldier will?
That fool didn't even need the wine
with the sleeping potion.
He would have slept all night without it."

But the youngest princess said,
"Let us look at him before we go,
just to be sure."

So they did.
The soldier's eyes were shut.
He didn't move.
All he did was snore.

"I told you," said the eldest.

Then she went to her bed
and clapped her hands three times.
At once the bed sank into the floor.
And the twelve princesses started down
a secret staircase
with the eldest leading the way.

The soldier lost no time.
He jumped from his bed
and threw on the cloak.
The old woman of the forest
had spoken the truth.
The moment he put on the cloak,
he became invisible.

Then he ran down the stairs,
right behind the youngest princess.
He was so close
he stepped on the hem of her gown.

"Someone is pulling my gown!" she cried.

"Don't be silly!" said the eldest.
"You must have caught it on a nail."

Down, down, down
they all went
till they were deep underground.

There the soldier found himself on a path
in a magical forest.
The trees sparkled
as if they were covered
with thousands of stars.

The soldier looked closely.
*The leaves were all of shimmering silver.*
"The king will never believe this!" he thought.
"I must take a branch to show him."

So he reached for a tiny branch.
But no sooner did he break it off
than the tree let out a great cry.

"What was that noise?" asked the youngest princess.

"Someone is blowing a trumpet
to welcome us," said the eldest.

Next they came to a forest
where the leaves were all of shining gold.
Then they reached a forest
where every tree had leaves
of glittering diamonds.

The soldier broke off a tiny branch
from a tree of gold
and a tree of diamonds.
And each time the tree let out a great cry.
"Something is wrong!" said the youngest princess.

"I told you," said the eldest.
"It's only a trumpet."

Soon they came to a large lake.
By the shore of the lake
there were twelve little boats.
In every boat sat a handsome prince.

Each princess stepped into a boat,
and the soldier sat beside the youngest.
"The boat seems heavy tonight," she said.
And the prince agreed.
He rowed and rowed
with all his might,
but the boat moved very slowly.

On the other side of the lake
stood a marble castle
lit from top to bottom.
The sounds of trumpets, flutes, and drums
rang through the open windows.

"Ah," thought the soldier,
"what merry music for dancing!"
Once inside the ballroom,
each prince danced with his princess.
The invisible soldier danced, too.
But, of course, no one could see him.

Then the soldier played a little game.
Whenever a princess held a cup of wine,
he drank from it.
By the time she put it to her lips,
the cup was almost empty.

"This is very strange," said the youngest princess.

But the eldest told her not to worry.

And so it went.
On and on they danced
till three in the morning.
Then their shoes were worn out
and they had to stop.

The princes rowed them back
across the lake.
This time the soldier sat
beside the eldest princess.

When they reached the shore,
the princesses said good-bye to their princes.
"We will return tomorrow night," they promised.

Then they slowly returned, back
through the forest of diamonds,
and the forests of gold and silver.

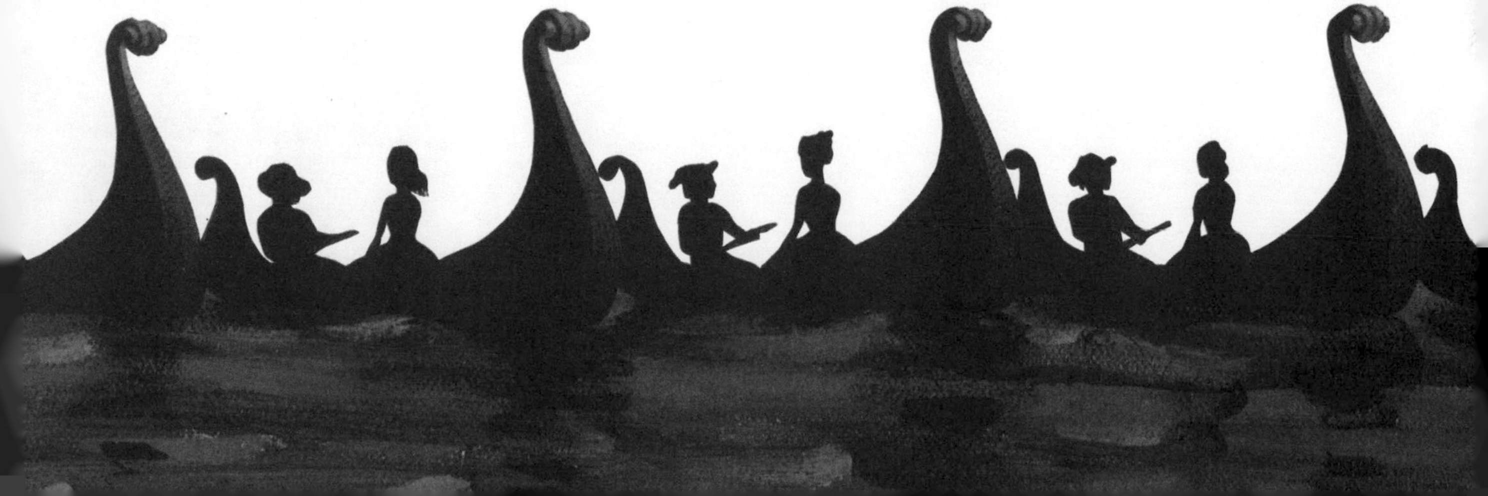

The moment they came to the secret stairs,
the invisible soldier ran ahead.
He hung up the cloak
and quickly got into bed.

By the time the twelve princesses
reached their room,
they heard him snoring loudly.

"We're safe," they whispered.
Then they took off their jewels and gowns
and put them away.
They kicked off their shoes,
lay down, and fell fast asleep.

The next morning the soldier said
nothing to the king.
He wanted to see more
of the magical world underground.

So he followed the princesses again
on the second and third nights.
Everything happened the same as before.
The princesses danced
till their shoes were full of holes.

But on the third night,
the soldier carried away
a golden cup to show the king.

The next morning it was time
for the soldier to give his answer.
So he took the three branches and the golden cup
and went before the king.

The twelve princesses listened behind the door
to hear what he would say.

"Do you know where my daughters go every night
and dance their shoes to pieces?" asked the king.

"Yes I do," said the soldier.
"They dance with twelve enchanted princes
in a castle underground."
And he told the king everything
that had happened.

"That's impossible!" cried the king.

"I have proof," said the soldier.
And he held out the three branches
and the golden cup.

At once the king called for his daughters.
"Has this soldier told me the truth?" he asked.

The twelve princesses bowed their heads.
"Yes," they whispered.

"Well! Well!" said the king.
"You are a very lucky man.
  Which of my daughters
  do you choose for a wife?"

"I'm not as young
  as I used to be," said the soldier.
"I will take the eldest."

So the wedding was held that very day.
And the soldier became heir to the kingdom
just as the king had promised.

But the twelve princes remained
under a magic spell for as many nights
as they had danced with the king's daughters.
And no one knows how long that was.

*To Glenn and Lyssa*
*—F.L.*

*To Joyce, Eva, and Daniel*
*—I.S.*

ISBN 0-590-41185-3

Text copyright © 1988 by Freya Littledale.
Illustrations copyright © 1988 by Isadore Seltzer.
All rights reserved. Published by Scholastic Inc.
Design by Meredith Dunham

12  11  10  9  8  7  6  5  4  3  2        8  9/8  0  1  2  3/9

Printed in the U.S.A.                     23

First Scholastic printing, August 1988